Oliver's Treehouse Friends

Written and illustrated by
Bruce Peardon

Published by the Association of Mouth and Foot Painting Artists
Copyright © MFPA
ISBN: 978-0-9565384-2-0
Designed by: Foster de Kretser Design Consultants fdk.co.uk

THIS BOOK
BELONGS TO...

Oliver was a five-year-old boy who lived with his mum and his dad in a lovely home, which was surrounded by tall eucalypt trees and bushland.

Oliver's dad was an airline pilot who was sometimes away for nearly a whole week, but when his dad was not working he would spend lots of days playing with Oliver. Every time an airplane would fly overhead, Oliver would always wave to it because he knew his dad would be able to see him and would be home soon.

Although Oliver had lots of friends at pre-school, he had no brothers and sisters and no young children as neighbours, so he sometimes played with pretend playmates.

Oliver's mum and dad knew their little boy had pretend friends, for sometimes when he was playing they could hear him talk to someone, but whenever they looked, they could only see Oliver. So they would look and smile and say, "Oliver is with his imaginary friends again."

One day a truck pulled up at Oliver's house and delivered a big load of timber, which made Oliver very curious. He asked his mum what the timber was for and she smiled and told him that his dad was going to do some work when he came home from flying.

When Oliver's dad arrived home for a three day break, he told Oliver he would need his help for he had to build something very important.

Oliver was so pleased that he was going to help his dad and happily worked all day handing his dad nails and holding the measuring tape, as slowly, the building took shape.

Then finally it was finished. It was the best looking treehouse a boy could ever have. It was built around a big gum tree and had a balcony, old ladder and even a window that Oliver's dad had bought at a second hand timber yard. Oliver hugged his mum and dad and thanked them for giving him such a lovely present.

It was getting quite late by the time the treehouse was completed so Oliver had just a short while to play in it before his mum called him in for his bath and dinner.

Working with his dad on the treehouse had made him very sleepy, so after dinner, Oliver brushed his teeth and was soon tucked up in bed. Then, excited with thoughts of what wonderful games he would play in his new cubby, he drifted off to sleep. But as Oliver slept there was all kinds of activity outside in the bush. Creatures who had slept, hidden away in the trees by day, were waking up and starting to search around for food. Animals and birds that do this are called nocturnal, they sleep in the daytime and then come out at night to eat and play.

High up in the tree a green tree-frog stirred from his daytime sleep and jumped from branch to branch. He looked around and then plopped down on the balcony of the treehouse thinking to himself that this would make a good spot to sit and wait for a passing insect that he would gobble up for his dinner.

Next a sugar-glider, which is a little possum that can spread open flaps between its front and back legs and glide from one tree to the other, landed on a branch and peered curiously at the treehouse and wondered what it could be.

Then a friendly old ringtail possum climbed up onto the treehouse balcony, cautiously sniffed around and deciding there was no danger, went inside.

"This would make an excellent place to sleep during the day," thought the ringtail. "After I have had my dinner, I think I will come back here."

And off he went in search of some food.

14

Early next morning, just as the dawn was breaking, a koala was looking for a nice tree in which to spend the whole day sleeping.

Now, as it happened, the tree around which Oliver's treehouse had been built was one of the koala's favourites. As the koala started to climb the tree, he noticed something strange had happened.

"What's happened to my tree?" thought the koala. He started to make grumpy noises and then noticed a ladder. Still grumbling he decided to climb the ladder to find out what was going on. You can imagine his surprise when he saw his mate, the ringtail possum, inside the treehouse.

"What are you doing in here?" asked Koala.

"I thought I'd sleep in here for the day," said Ringtail, "it is so nice and sheltered."

"Good idea!" said Koala, "I think I'll join you."

So the friends set about making themselves comfortable for the day and soon they were drifting off to sleep.

Oliver was awoken by the sound of a laughing kookaburra, and when he looked out of his window he saw the bird sitting on the balcony rail of his treehouse. He was immediately filled with excitement at the thought of playing in his treehouse and quickly got dressed and went down to have breakfast.

When he'd finished his breakfast he took the little telescope his dad had given him and went out to his treehouse. It was Saturday, so he had all day to play.

Oliver happily climbed the ladder and thought that today he might be a pirate and look for tall ships through his telescope.

As he was about to go inside his treehouse he heard a grumbling sound. At first he was a little frightened, but then he decided to have a look at what was making the noise.

He could not believe his eyes when he saw the koala and the possum. They seemed very scared of him, so he said softly, "Don't worry, I won't hurt you. My name is Oliver, what's yours?"

The animals still seemed nervous, so Oliver said, "Would you like some gum leaves?" He had seen koalas eating gum leaves when his parents had taken him to the koala sanctuary. So he went outside and plucked some overhanging leaves and offered them to the koala.

Very timidly the koala took the leaves and Oliver gave a big smile.

"Now what would you like to eat?" he said to the possum. Then he remembered his granddad had a pet possum and he fed it bits of apple and bread. So Oliver clambered down the tree and ran into the kitchen to get some food for the possum.

Oliver's mum was busy in the laundry when he went inside, so he grabbed some toast scraps and hurried back to the treehouse.

The possum took the scraps and ate them with relish
and Oliver was so pleased that he said, "I think I will
name you two Blinky Bill and Hush, because those are
names from my two favourite books, 'Possum Magic'
and 'The Adventures of Blinky Bill'."

They didn't seem to mind Oliver anymore and soon
they had fallen asleep, so Oliver went outside with
his telescope to see if he could see other creatures
in the trees.

It wasn't long before he spotted a very strange looking bird. It was a tawny frogmouth owl. It was so well hidden it looked just like the bark of a tree. It seemed to sense Oliver was looking at it and it opened an eye and gave him a wary look. He thought how much it looked like Oscar the Grouch out of 'Sesame Street'.

Oliver kept looking and it was then that he saw the weirdest creature of all hidden in the dense foliage in the gully at the back of his yard. It was a Queensland tube-nosed bat. Oliver wasn't sure what it was, but it reminded him of a kitten sleeping in a bag.

Oliver kept watching the many birds darting through the trees and the morning passed so quickly that it was soon lunchtime. Oliver's mother surprised him by bringing his lunch, served with a picnic plate and cup, out to the treehouse. He had an orange drink, a chicken sandwich and a pear.

Oliver ate what he could and then left the remainder on the plate. Almost as soon as he had left it, a cheeky magpie flew down and took a piece of leftover chicken.

Then just as suddenly, two beautiful rainbow
lorikeets fluttered onto the balcony and
screeching and chatting started to eat what
was left of the pear.

Oliver was thrilled at the lovely birds and
he wondered if other children had so many
wonderful creatures in their backyards.

Oliver played every day in his treehouse and took scraps and leaves to his friends. One day his mum said, "Who is it I sometimes hear you talking to in your treehouse, Oliver?"

"Oh they're just my friends Blinky Bill and Hush," replied Oliver and went off to play.

Mum smiled and thought, "Oliver! He's always playing with his imaginary friends."

One day Oliver's mum had to go out and wouldn't be home until late, so his dad was looking after him. His dad was very tired because he'd come home from a long flight and so in the late afternoon he went to sleep whilst he and Oliver were watching a rugby match on television.

Oliver felt a bit tired too, but he thought he would go and see his mates in the treehouse and he took his snuggle rug and pillow with him in case he wanted to lie down. He also took an apple to share with the possum and, leaving his dad quietly snoring in the lounge chair, he crept out.

Dad woke as Oliver's mum came home and said as he stretched, "I must have nodded off for a while."

"Where is Oliver?" asked Mum.

"In his room I suppose," said Dad.

They searched the house and when they could not find Oliver, Dad decided to look outside.

"But it's dark!" said Mum,

"I'd better get the torch and have a look," said Dad worriedly. Dad got the torch and he and Mum went outside. They called out but there was no answer. They looked everywhere, but Oliver was nowhere to be found. Finally Dad decided to check the treehouse thinking that perhaps Oliver had gone there for a nap.

So he climbed the treehouse ladder and when he shone his torch inside, he couldn't believe what he saw. He called softly for Mum to come up the ladder.

"Have a look at this," he whispered, and smiled.

There was Oliver, sound asleep. But he wasn't alone. For right there was a koala cuddled up beside him and a possum sleepily peeping around the side of the gum tree which grew through the middle of the house.

"My goodness!" exclaimed Mum putting her hand to her mouth.

"He told me about his friends but I thought they were just made up," she said.

At that moment Oliver and Koala woke up. Koala gave a yawn and a grumble and headed out of the door, closely followed by the possum.

"I thought that when you said you had friends in the treehouse, Oliver, they were just pretend ones," said his mother.

Oliver sat up and said, "Kids don't have pretend friends, Mum, it's just that grown ups can't always see them."

Mum and Dad laughed and Dad said, "I think you're right Oliver… Now, come on, let's go and have some dinner and you can tell us all about your treehouse friends."

Bruce Peardon

Bruce Peardon was born in Brisbane, Queensland, Australia in 1945. While serving with the Royal Australian Navy he was seriously injured in a motor accident. The severe spinal damage resulted in total paralysis from his neck down.

Bruce had always been interested in art and naturally progressed to painting by holding the brush in his mouth. He mastered this unique skill and became a member of the Association of Mouth and Foot Painting Artists.

He continued to develop his skills, both in watercolour and oils, and his art is held in high esteem. His works hang in private and public collections in his own country and overseas.

Bruce gave tirelessly of his time and expertise to aspiring young artists who had lost the use of their arms. He worked hard for the advancement of the Association of Mouth and Foot Painting Artists.

Bruce died suddenly in May 2001. He is survived by his wife Chris and their son Ben. His death left a void in the lives of all who knew him. He will be remembered for his friendship, his belief in the youth of the world and his unbridled love of life.